First published in 2016 in Great Britain by
Barrington Stoke Ltd
18 Walker Street, Edinburgh, EH3 7LP

www.barringtonstoke.co.uk

This story was first published in a different form as
Countdown (Heinemann Young Books, 1996)

Text © 1996 Anne Fine
Illustrations © 2016 Vicki Gausden

The moral right of Anne Fine and Vicki Gausden to be
identified as the author and illustrator of this work has been
asserted in accordance with the Copyright, Designs and
Patents Act, 1988

A CIP catalogue record for this book is available
from the British Library upon request

ISBN: 978-1-78112-507-6

Printed in China by Leo

This book has dyslexia friendly features

Out for the Count

Anne Fine

Illustrated by Vicki Gausden

Barrington Stoke

For Teddy

Contents

Chapter 1

A Perfect Cage

11.04 a.m.

Hugo James MacFee sat on the newspaper spread all over his empty bedroom.

"So, can I have a gerbil?" he asked his father.

"No," his father said as he painted round the last corner.

"I promise I'd look after it properly."

"I'm sure you would," his father said. "But that's not the point. Think of the gerbil. How would you like to spend your whole life stuck in a cage?"

"I'd let it out," Hugo said.

"But you're at school all day."

Hugo counted up on his fingers. "I'm only out for seven hours," he said.

His father painted over the last of the yellow with the new blue.

"It's a very long time to sit in a boring old cage all by yourself, with nothing to do," he said.

"I could give it things to play with while I'm gone."

"That might not be enough to keep it happy."

"But it would be clean and safe and comfy."

His father looked around at the four fresh blue walls. "This bedroom's clean and safe and comfy," he said. "A perfect cage, in fact, for someone of your size. But you wouldn't want to spend seven hours in here, all by yourself."

"I'd be all right," said Hugo.

His father dropped the paint brush into the tin. "Prove it," he said. "Spend the day in here."

Hugo looked round the empty room. "In here? The whole day?"

"For seven hours," his father said. "The time that you'd be out on a normal school day."

Hugo looked at his watch. It was eleven in the morning.

"Start at twelve," said his father. "Take an hour to get organised, then see if you can stick it. Midday until evening. Twelve o'clock till seven."

"And if I do it, can I have a gerbil?" Hugo asked.

His father picked up the paint rags. "If you can do it," he said, "I'll not just bring your furniture back in. I'll bring a gerbil too."

"It's a deal," Hugo said. "Let's make sure our watches say the same. I make it 11.04."

Mr MacFee set his watch. Hugo set his watch too.

"So," Mr MacFee said. "It's 11.04. One plate of food. One bottle of water. Three of your old toys. And all the newspaper that's spread over the floor. Is that a deal?"

"See you at twelve," said Hugo. "I'll be ready to go."

Chapter 2

Ready?

11.58 a.m.

Mr MacFee closed his hand round the door knob and looked at his watch.

"Ready?" he asked.

Hugo checked everything. His water bottle was here, his food plate there, and the three things he'd taken from the toy box were spread out in front of him on the floor.

"Ready," he told his father. "Are you going to lock me in?"

"No, I am not," his father said. "I don't believe in locking any animal in a cage – not even a human one like you."

And he just shut the door.

Chapter 3

A Box of Bricks

12.01 p.m.

Hugo looked around what he now thought of as his nice new cage.

Soft breaths of air waltzed in the open window. The one bare light bulb hung from the clean white ceiling.

The walls shone a perfect Harebell Blue. Across the floor lay a square sea of newspapers. On top of that lay the three things that Hugo had borrowed from Charlotte's toy box.

1. The dancing monkey on a stick.

2. Wee Grey Ghostie.

3. The box of baby bricks.

Hugo had taken the monkey on a stick because Charlotte wouldn't let him touch it when she was around. He'd chosen Wee Grey Ghostie because she was his favourite puppet when he was young.

And he'd picked up the brick box because he'd heard his mother say a thousand times that you could fill a

child's room with expensive toys, but when it came to keeping them busy for hours and hours, you couldn't beat a box of bricks.

So. Was she right?

Hugo built a tower.

Then he built a house.

He built a viaduct. And then a rather fancy archway that fell down.

And then a prison wall.

Then he was bored.

He took Wee Grey Ghostie and made her peer over his prison wall. She looked this way and that.

"Whooooooo," he made her say. "Whooooo. Whoooo. Whooooo."

Then he was bored.

He took the monkey on a stick and made it flip over and over.

"Hi, Ghostie," he made the monkey say.

"Whooooo," said Wee Grey Ghostie.

"Look at me."

"Whoooo."

"Backward flip. Up and over.
Hanging in the air."

"Whooooooo."

But Wee Grey Ghostie sounded a bit bored.

Hugo MacFee packed the bricks back in their box and laid the puppet ghost on top. He leaned the monkey on a stick against the lid.

As soon as he got out, he'd tell his mother she was wrong. A box of bricks was just as boring as a puppet ghost and a monkey on a stick.

How long had Hugo been in here, then? Hugo peered at his watch.

12.31 p.m.

Just under six and a half more hours to go.

Chapter 4

Chocolate Biscuits

12.32 p.m.

Hugo read the newspaper. It wasn't easy. Great splatters of white paint had fallen on it from the ceiling. That made it hard to read.

New rules for banks he made out. Then **Shoe sales on the up and up**. Boring. **Shares fall after fears**. But fears of what, he didn't know, because that was now a big white blob of paint. He tried to pick it off, but only tore the paper.

He tried another patch.

Massive deposits ... new share price.

What was all that about?

Boring in spades.

He crawled across the floor, with his nose to the paper. There it was, all around him – business news.

Nothing worth reading. No **Killer Shark Eats Family of Four**. No **Wind Snatches Wig off Beauty Queen**. No **More Haunted House Horrors**.

When Hugo grew up, he would buy a proper paper, not the 'Financial Times'. He'd speak to his father about it the moment he got out of here.

When would that be?

Hugo looked at his watch.

In six hours and twenty-one minutes.

Less than an hour gone. It seemed like weeks.

12.41 p.m.

So was he hungry yet?

Hugo had a little think. He wasn't hungry yet. He'd had a proper breakfast. Then, just in case, an early lunch. His orange sat on the plate. His sandwich waited. And his three chocolate biscuits lay in a pile. He planned to eat his snack at 4.30 p.m. Then, when he got out at seven, he'd have his supper. His mother had promised to keep it warm.

That was the plan. Hugo looked at the plate again.

Orange. Sandwich. And two chocolate biscuits.

Two? Only *two*?

Hugo stared. Where had the third one *gone*? Oh no! Look! Biscuit crumbs on his chest! He hadn't even noticed he was eating it. Only 12.44 p.m. What a *waste*. If he'd been thinking, he'd have taken more time with that chocolate biscuit.

Chapter 5

All at Sea

12.47 p.m.

Hugo rocked back and forth on the floor. The walls swayed with him, blue as sky. Sky all around. No, sea. Sea all around him. He was on a raft. A speckled, printed raft.

The blobs of paint were droppings from the seagulls. There was no land in sight. Nothing but sea for miles and miles. Perhaps a dolphin would come. Maybe a whale or even a shiver of sharks.

What was that strange shape over there that looked like a paint scraper on the floor, but could easily be ... Shark!

The sandwich went flying, as Hugo
snatched up the plate and paddled with
all his might. He gritted his teeth. "Save
me!" he hissed. "Oh save me, someone!
Is there no one there?"

Around him, the seagulls cried.
The light bulb sun beat down. And a
soft breeze crept over the window sill,
over the waves and raft, to cool Hugo's
fevered brow.

He paddled hard. He paddled even harder.

"Oh, for a sight of land!" he cried. "Six weeks! Six long, long weeks adrift. My stores so low that I have only a sandwich, and an orange, and two ship's biscuits left. If no boat passes, I will be sure to die!"

His paddling grew more frantic.

"Help!" he cried. "Help me! – Oh, oh, help!"

But no help came.

Hugo paddled on through the waves and then, when he was tired out and there was no hope left, he just gave up and ate his only sandwich.

12.59 p.m.

A man stuck on a raft on a burning sea will soon go mad.

Hugo went mad.

"Ghostie," he whispered. "Ghostie, can you remember back to when you were not Charlotte's toy, but mine?"

Wee Ghostie nodded. How could she forget?

"And you were white?"

Wee Ghostie hung her head.

"Well," Hugo confessed. "You know that day Mum stuffed you in the washing machine by mistake, and I sat and watched you going round and round, until you went grey?"

Wee Ghostie nodded again.

"That was my fault," Hugo admitted. "I was the one who dropped you in the washing basket by mistake. If I'd done what I was told, and sorted the washing better, you wouldn't have gone all lumpy and grey."

Wee Ghostie hung her lumpy grey head.

"Sorry," said Hugo. "I am really sorry."

Wee Ghostie said not a word.

Hugo cheered up. "Still," he said, "I feel a whole lot better, just for telling you."

Wee Ghostie stared at him.

Chapter 6

Dreams of Escape

1.03 p.m.

Hugo leaned out of the window as far as he dared. If he could slip his hand around the metal strut that held the gutter up, he could swing over to the drainpipe.

Then he could shin down that as far as the tree. If the big branch held, he could slide down as far as Mr Foster's wall, crawl along that, and then let himself down on the wheelie bins.

Or he could rip his clothes into long shreds, knot them into a rope, and tie it to the window catch. He could slither down and jump. He'd have to make sure that he missed the rose bush. Then he would land on the grass, next to the cat's bowl.

Or he could climb up on the guttering, balance along and then crawl up the roof, over the top, and down the other side, on to the porch.

Or he could just walk out the door, of course ... But not for – Hugo looked at his watch – five hours and fifty minutes.

Hugo watched the numbers on his watch face flash and change.

Five hours and forty-nine minutes.
He watched them change again.

Five hours and forty-eight minutes.

A gerbil wouldn't have a watch, of
course, to count the minutes. All that
a gerbil could do was prowl around his
nice new cage as time ticked by.

1.13 p.m.

Hugo prowled around his new blue room. The smell of paint was strongest in the corner that Dad had painted last. Sunlight fell on the furthest wall, to make the paint there look lighter.

When the sun dropped behind the tree there might be shadows that Hugo could watch to pass the time. But not until then. And that was hours away.

1.17 p.m.

Hugo picked up the orange and tossed it in the air.

Once.

Twice.

Again.

Then, bored, he sniffed at it.

The smell of orange peel was sharper than he'd thought. He scraped it with his nail to make it smell even more strong, and then he lay down and held the orange to his nose.

Now he was lying under an orange tree. He was in Spain. If he opened his eyes he'd see a terrace and a swimming pool.

He'd inch his way across the burning tiles and slither over the edge, into the crystal water.

The cool, cool blue would close over his head and he would twist and turn under the sunlit droplets.

Splash, splash!

Free as a fish!

No. Hugo was an eagle now.

From way, way up, he'd spot the orange peeking from its branch, and he would swoop down to knock it from the tree, from sheer high spirits.

The sharp fizz taste would smear his beak and send him wheeling up again, into high blue skies.

Flap, flap!

Free as a bird!

But he was here under a clean white ceiling, trapped in on all four sides by Harebell Blue walls.

Beneath him lapped not silky water, but the grubby old 'Financial Times'.

On holiday, his father said, a dozen times a day, "This is the life!"

'And this,' thought Hugo, 'isn't. It's not the life at all.'

Chapter 7

An Ear to the Door

1.29 p.m.

First Hugo ripped out the word HELP. (He found it in a headline – HELP FOR SALES.)

Then he tore round the ME (in MERCHANDISE).

He found ...

an I (in INTEREST RATES)

an AM (in AMERICAN SHARES)

the letters TRA (in TRADE)

a spare P (in PENSIONS)

and then a PED (in PEDESTRIAN CROSSING).

Last of all, Hugo found the biggest, thickest blob of paint and picked it off. He was in luck – it was still sticky. He used it to glue his message to the blankest patch of paper he could find (which was a bit of bare wall in a photo of the Manager of Tesco).

His fingers were covered with white paint, but he had done it.

HELP. I AM TRAPPED.

What did he need now? An empty bottle, of course.

Hugo tipped back his head and drank his water, every last drop of it. He rolled his message up and pushed it in the bottle. Then he crawled to the door.

Footsteps!

Hugo was sure that he had heard footsteps coming up the stairs. Was it his mum? Or his dad? It couldn't be Charlotte. She was still at Granny's house.

He put his ear to the door.

Thud, thud.

His heart beat with excitement.

Thud. **Thud**. **Thud**.

The steps drew nearer. Then they passed the door. He heard a rattle further along the hall. Someone was going into his parents' bedroom now.

It could be either of them. Hard to tell. Hugo waited with his ear pressed up against the door for quite a while. And then he heard it all again, but in reverse. *Rattle.*

Then **thud, thud, thud** along the hall – right outside his door!

Then **thud, thud** down the stairs. The sound faded away.

Hugo leaned back against the door. He was worn out from all the excitement.

It was the most dramatic thing that had happened in – Hugo looked at his watch – nearly two hours. It was 1.56 p.m.

1.59 p.m.

"Right," Hugo told his brain. "Stop thinking. Empty yourself. Go blank. Go totally blank."

Right at the back of his brain, a silent voice reminded him, "Let's not forget our manners. Try saying 'please'."

'Please,' Hugo thought. 'Please!'

But then he wondered why he felt he had to suck up to one small bit of himself. You wouldn't say "please" to a toenail, would you? Or to a knee? Why should your brain get all the fancy treatment? Was it fair?

Hugo tried to unsay "please".

"I didn't mean that," Hugo told his brain. "It doesn't count. We'll start again."

He took a deep breath.

"Right," he said. "Stop thinking. Empty yourself. Go totally blank."

"You mind your manners, Hugo," said his brain.

"My manners are none of your business."

"I think they are," his brain said.

"Who says?" asked Hugo.

"I do," his brain replied.

"But you're just me," said Hugo. "You're nothing but my brain. And if it weren't for me, you wouldn't be here, would you?"

"And if it weren't for me," his brain snapped, "you wouldn't be here either. So snubs to you."

"And snubs to you," Hugo snapped back.

"With big brass knobs on."

"And with double return."

Hugo jumped to his feet.

"I'm going mad!" he cried out loud.

"Serves you right!" Hugo's brain crowed.

"Shut up!" Hugo shouted.

"Shut up yourself," his brain snarled.

"You shut up first."

"No, you."

"You started it."

"No, I did not."

Hugo knew that his brain was right. He'd started it himself by trying to tell his brain what it should do.

"Call it quits?" Hugo offered.

"Yes, quits," his brain agreed.

It took a bit of time and both the chocolate biscuits, but in the end the brain piped down in Hugo's head.

By 2.09 p.m. he felt more himself again.

Chapter 8

Losing Track of Time

2.13 p.m.

Hugo sang 'Flower of Scotland' to the light bulb at the top of his voice. Then he sang 'When My Sugar Walks Down the Street' (his father's favourite). He sang a mix of nursery rhymes from the book his mum had forced him to pass down to Charlotte.

He sang all the jingles from the TV that he could think of, and the song from 'The Scooby Doo Show'. Then the first verse – all that he could remember – of Granny's favourite carol, 'Ye Holy Angels Bright'.

After that, Hugo sang 'Flower of Scotland' all over again. Then he was bored.

He sat and twiddled his thumbs as he waited for the end numbers to change on his watch face.

2.30 ... 2.31 ... 2.32 ...

Hugo lost track of time for a bit – how did it get to 2.37? – and then he tried to pick the last of the sticky white paint off the tips of his fingers. But it didn't work.

He lay back and imagined he was drowning. Down, down into the salty darkness he would go, under the folding billows of the sea.

His hair would ripple like weeds, and his eyes would blaze like underwater headlamps. Hugo sat up with a jolt and looked at his watch. 2.41 p.m.

Chapter 9

A Wise Decision

2.43 p.m.

Hugo James MacFee took a quick vote on it.

The monkey on a stick was all for giving up. Wee Grey Ghostie was happy either way. And Hugo didn't give the bricks a say.

The light bulb said nothing but it did stare down as Hugo announced the official result.

"In favour of staying – none. In favour of leaving – two." That was settled, then. They were leaving.

Hugo picked up Grey Ghostie and the monkey on a stick and walked to the door. (He abandoned the bricks.)

He checked his watch face one last time.

2.47 p.m.

Hugo bumped into his father on the stairs. His father looked at him. Then he looked at the tips of Hugo's fingers.

"I hope you haven't left sticky white fingerprints all over my fresh painted walls," he said.

Hugo ignored him.

Mr MacFee gave his son another long, steady look. "Would you like me to help you carry your stuff back in?" he asked.

Hugo shook his head. "No, thank you," he told his father. "Not right now. I thought I'd go outside and play."

"A wise decision," said his father.

He stood and watched as Hugo went down the stairs and out of the back door, into the wind and the sun.

It was 2.49 p.m. and Hugo James MacFee was free.